Read slowly, then…
Close your eyes
See the images
Savor the wor(l)d
Imagine the future
Feel the colors
Hear the sounds
Smell the paper
Touch the story
Enjoy

minedition
North American edition published 2014 by Michael Neugebauer Publishing Ltd. Hong Kong

Text copyright © 2009 by Kate Westerlund
Illustrations copyright © 2009 by Robert Ingpen
Rights arranged with "minedition" Rights and Licensing AG, Zurich, Switzerland.
Michael Neugebauer Publishing Ltd., Unit 23, 7F, Kowloon Bay Industrial Centre,
15 Wang Hoi Road, Kowloon Bay, Hong Kong. e-mail: info@minedition.com
This book was printed in April 2014 at L.Rex Printing Co Ltd 3/F., Blue Box Factory Building,
25 Hing Wo Street, Tin Wan, Aberdeen, Hong Kong, China
Typesetting in Papyrus
Library of Congress Cataloging-in-Publication Data available upon request.

ISBN 978-988-8240-80-7

10 9 8 7 6 5 4 3 2 1
First impression

For more information please visit our website: www.minedition.com

If You Wish

by Kate Westerlund
Art by Robert Ingpen

minedition

"This is boring," said Willow.

"Why don't you read?" said a gruff voice.

"Who said that?"

"I did, of course."

"But I can't see you," said Willow.

"Where's your imagination?" said the voice.

"Why don't you read?"

"I've read all my books."

"You can read a book more than once, you know. You might even find a book inside the book."

"A what?"

"There's always another story. When you read a book again and let your imagination take over, it can take you to new stories, so it's like a book inside the book!"

"Are you real or are you just inside my head?"

"What's inside your head is real, isn't it?" said the voice.

"I guess so!"

"Then use your imagination and you'll see me at the edge of the park," said the scratchy voice.

Willow squinted and tried hard to imagine.

"Hello, it seems you do have imagination," said Tally.

"You look exactly like I imagined," she said, "even the scratchy voice."

"I beg your pardon, Tally always looks as you imagine, but a scratchy voice?"

"Please, tell me more about the book inside the book," said Willow.

"First tell me how you want to travel," said Tally.

"You must imagine something!"

Willow closed her eyes to concentrate.

Tally laughed.
"Carousel-travel, what a marvellous idea!"

"Perhaps all you need is a bit
  of practice," said Tally.
"Let's try."
  The carousel started to move.
  As the music got faster and faster,
  so did the carousel.
  It was a blur as it whirled,
  and then it slowed to a stop.

There were children on the horses.

"There's a spot for you on Linnet," said Tally.

"Will the others come with us?" asked Willow.

"No, they are on their way to other adventures," said Tally.

"Let's start with a book you have read.
The words brought you to the story the first time;
now let your imagination continue the journey."
The carousel started again, around and around,
whirling until it was a blur.

"Hold on tight, we're about to take off."

"Tally?"

"No, I'm Linnet," said the horse.

"You imagined a flying horse, didn't you?"

"But you can talk," said Willow.

"Don't all flying horses?" asked Linnet.

"We'll only have time for a few pages, but it should be enough. Do you have the book in mind?"

"Yes," said Willow.

"Now think about it. Imagine it. There'll be a blur and a whirl, so hang on."

"It's the marketplace from the beginning of the book," said Willow.
"But it is not just a picture anymore.
 The people are moving. It's real."

"What did you expect? Now imagine something new," said Linnet.
 Willow concentrated.

"Look, there I am, playing with the children, just like I imagined," said Willow.

"May I imagine something else, please?"

"Alright, select another page," said Linnet.

"I'm ready," said Willow.

There was a blur and a whirl and...

"I imagined we'd be small, just like in Wonderland. I wanted a garden
filled with flowers. And it worked, I did it. Isn't it beautiful?
Can I add something else?" asked Willow.
"If you wish," said Linnet.
Willow closed her eyes and imagined.

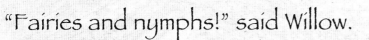

"Fairies and nymphs!" said Willow.

"Willow, our time is running short," said Linnet.

"Do we have time for one more page, please?" asked Willow.

"I know exactly what I want to imagine."

Linnet whinnied and there was
a blur and a whirl.

"Draaaagons? Willow, you could have warned me!"
"Sorry," said Willow. "I always thought the castle needed dragons."

"It's time," said Linnet.
"I know," said Willow,
"and there will be a blur and a whirl."

Willow saw the trees on the edge of the park.

"Now you know what's possible," said Linnet.

"But what if I ..." She didn't have a chance to finish.

Linnet was once again a carousel horse.

"Oh Tally, it was amazing, when can I do it again?"

"Whenever you wish!" said Tally.

"Will you and Linnet be here the next time?"

"I don't think you'll need us, but if you do…"

"I know, I know, just imagine, and there'll be a blur and a whirl!"

Tally and Linnet were gone.
The carousel and the park had disappeared too.
Willow found her stack of books.
"There are books inside these books, just waiting for you,"
 she said in a scratchy, Tally kind of voice, "if you wish."

"Of course I wish! Oh Tally, I can hardly wait."